Arrivals

For my dad,
who taught me
how to draw
helicopters in
church when
I was nine

Departures

Thanks to
Mr. Chuck Telles
of American
Airlines at PHL

Balzer + Bray is an imprint of HarperCollins Publishers. Everything Goes: In the Air. Copyright © 2012 by Brian Biggs. All rights reserved. Manufactured in China. No part of this book may be used or reproduced in any manner whatsoever without written permission except in the case of brief quotations embodied in critical articles and reviews. For information address HarperCollins Children's Books, a division of HarperCollins Publishers, 195 Broadway, New York, NY 10007. www.harpercollinschildrens.com

Library of Congress Cataloging-in-Publication Data is available.
ISBN 978-0-06-195810-6

Typography by Dana Fritts and Brian Biggs
17 18 19 20 SCP 10 9 8 7 6 5 4 3
❖ First Edition

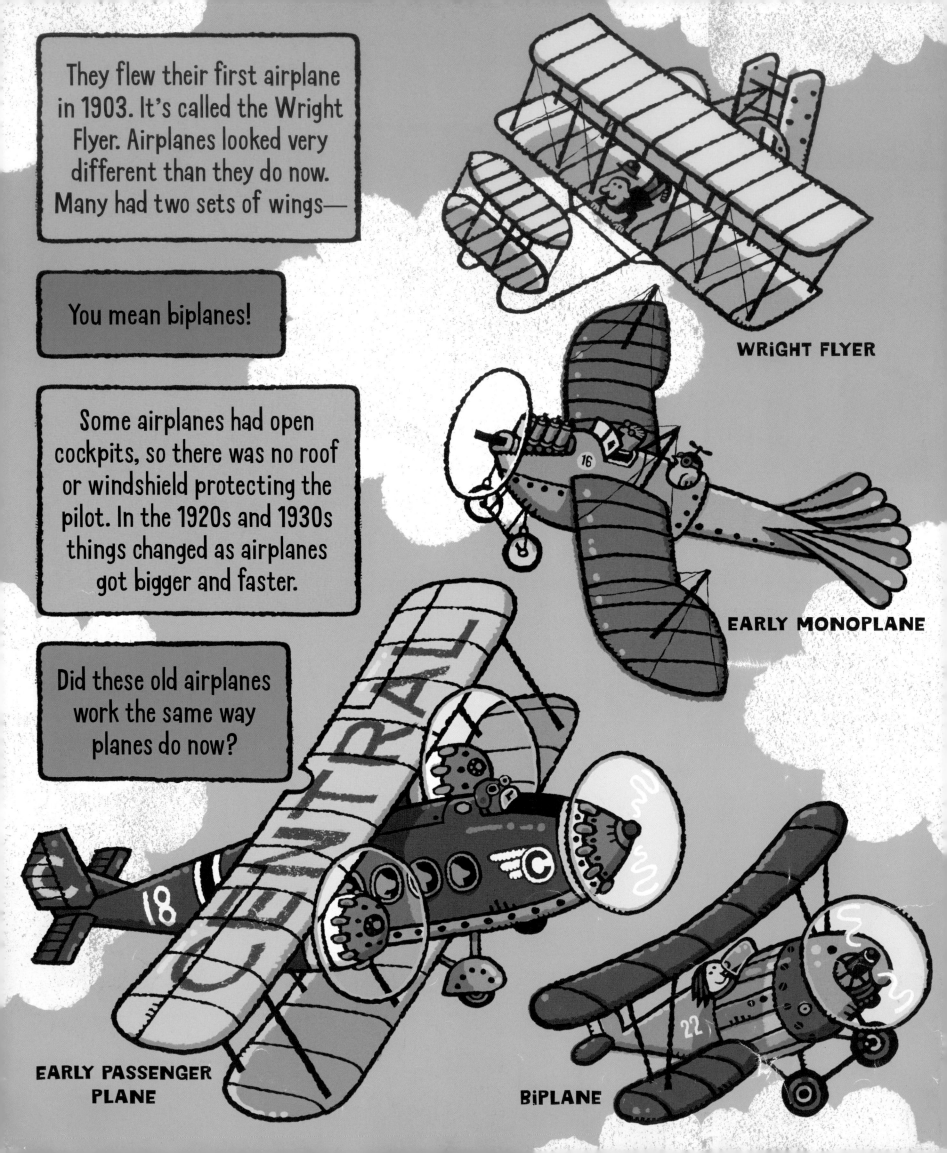

They flew their first airplane in 1903. It's called the Wright Flyer. Airplanes looked very different than they do now. Many had two sets of wings—

You mean biplanes!

Some airplanes had open cockpits, so there was no roof or windshield protecting the pilot. In the 1920s and 1930s things changed as airplanes got bigger and faster.

Did these old airplanes work the same way planes do now?

WRIGHT FLYER

EARLY MONOPLANE

EARLY PASSENGER PLANE

BIPLANE

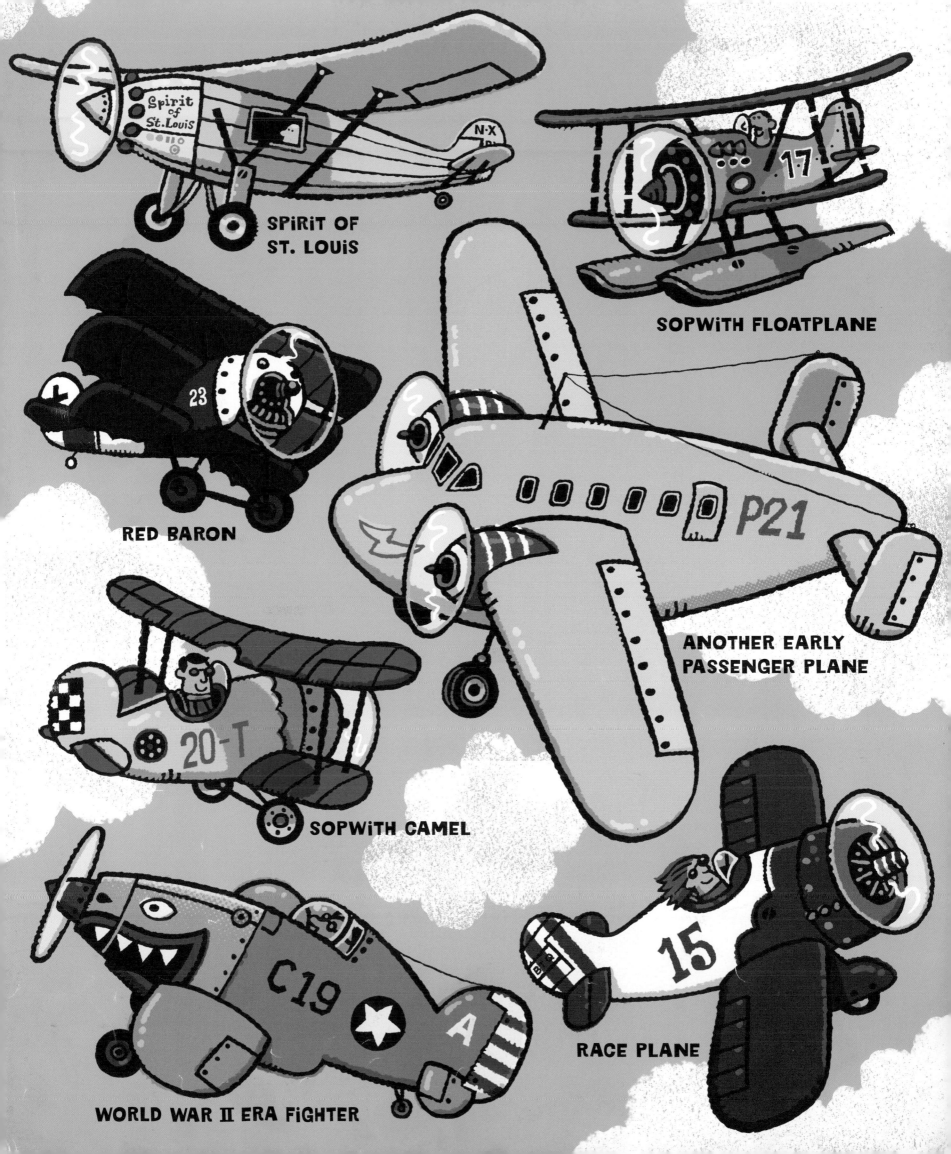

SPIRIT OF ST. LOUIS

SOPWiTH FLOATPLANE

RED BARON

ANOTHER EARLY PASSENGER PLANE

SOPWiTH CAMEL

WORLD WAR II ERA FIGHTER

RACE PLANE

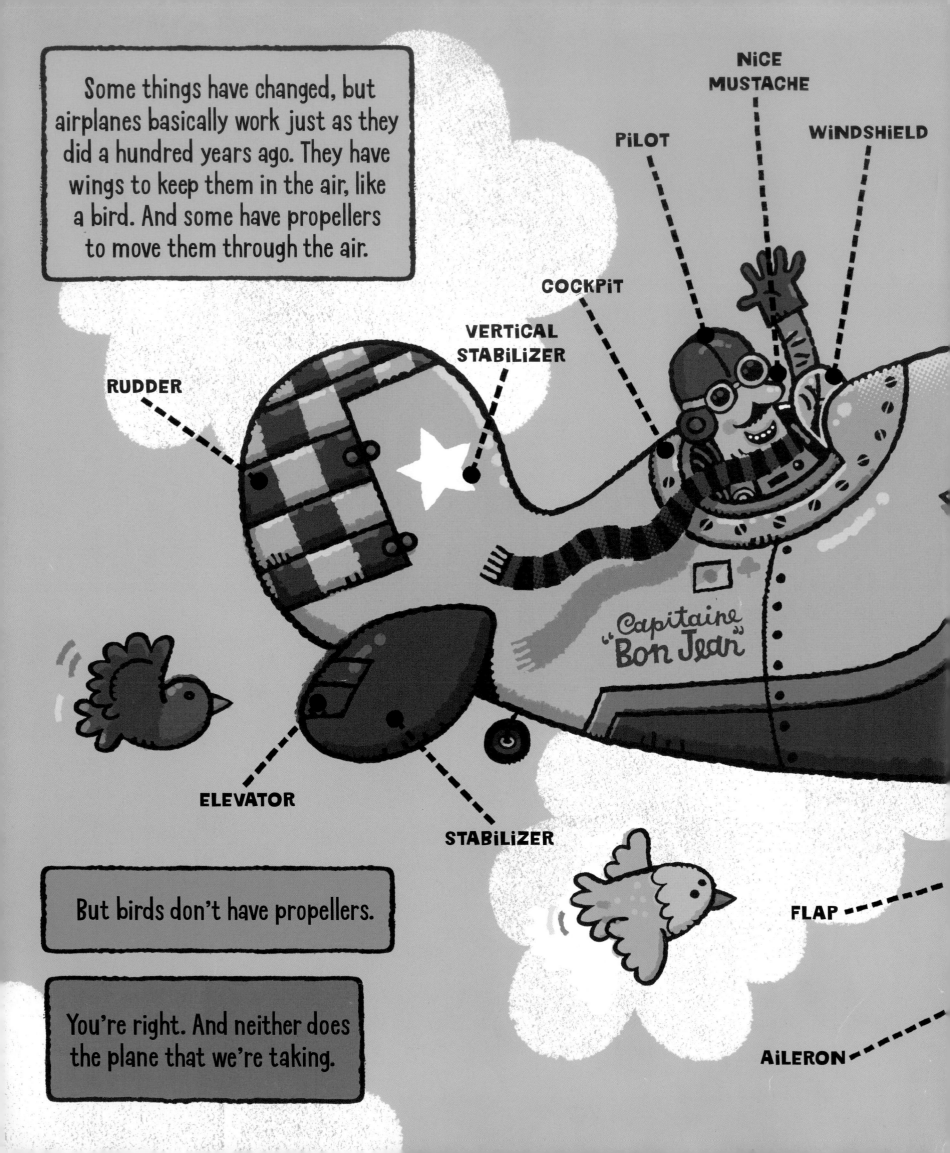

Some things have changed, but airplanes basically work just as they did a hundred years ago. They have wings to keep them in the air, like a bird. And some have propellers to move them through the air.

But birds don't have propellers.

You're right. And neither does the plane that we're taking.

NICE MUSTACHE

PILOT

WINDSHIELD

COCKPIT

VERTICAL STABILIZER

RUDDER

"Capitaine" Bon Jean

ELEVATOR

STABILIZER

FLAP

AILERON

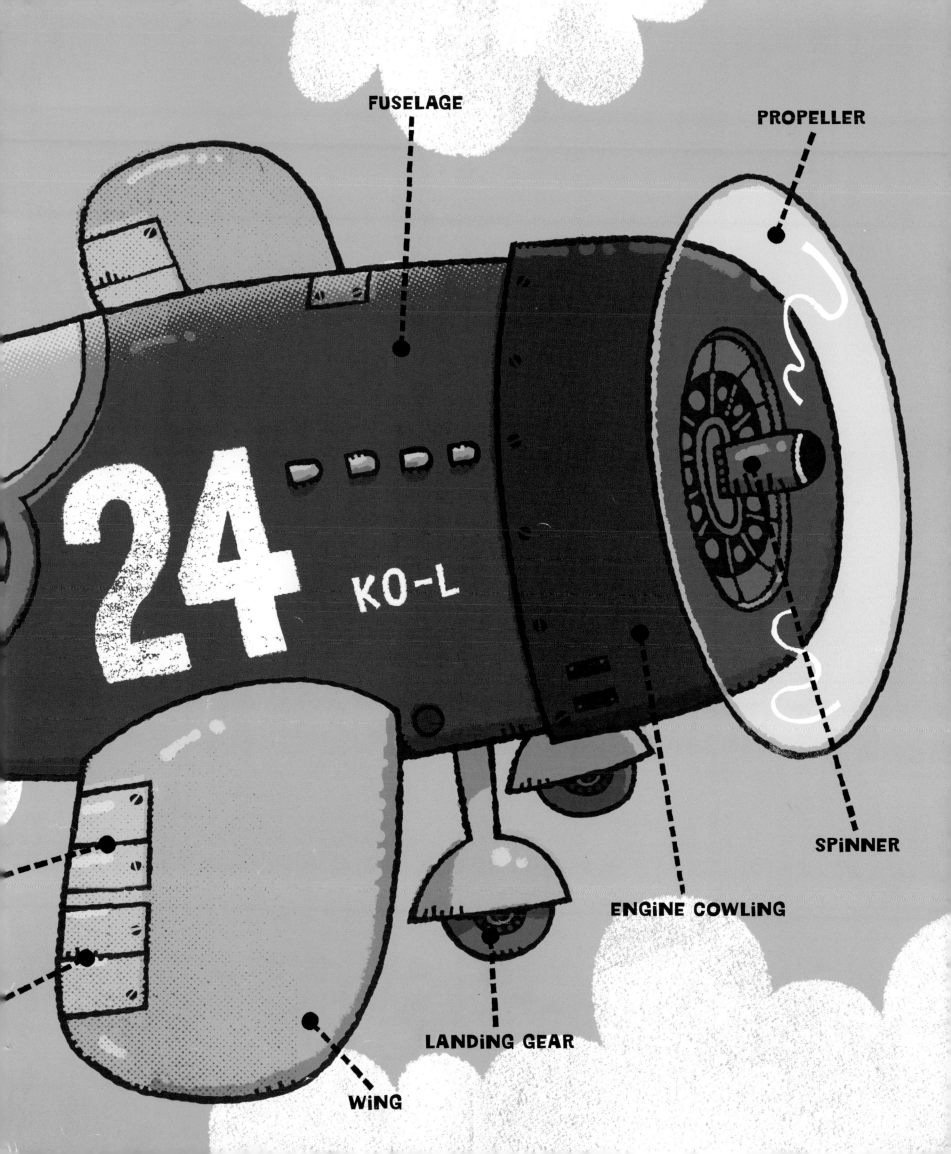

MILITARY JET

USA-40

PRIVATE PLANE
(GLIDER PULLER)

PG34

GLIDER

ALR-43P

COMPANY JET

RL42-N

What kinds of jobs
do airplanes have?

Some carry passengers,
just like our plane, but they are
smaller and made to fly shorter
distances. Some are made to
work on farms, to help take
care of crops. Some airplanes do
tricks or carry cargo, like a truck.

Did you know that some
airplanes can land on water?
Just in case there isn't
enough room for a runway.

CROP DUSTER

CD39

The propeller on a helicopter acts like the wings on an airplane—the propeller creates the lift that keeps it in the air.

ROTOR

TAIL BOOM

TAIL ROTOR

RTH54

ELEVATOR

What does the little propeller on a helicopter's tail do?

It's what helps helicopters turn. This combination allows them to hover in the air over one place. This makes them very useful for certain jobs that airplanes can't do. Helicopters can even land on the roofs of buildings!

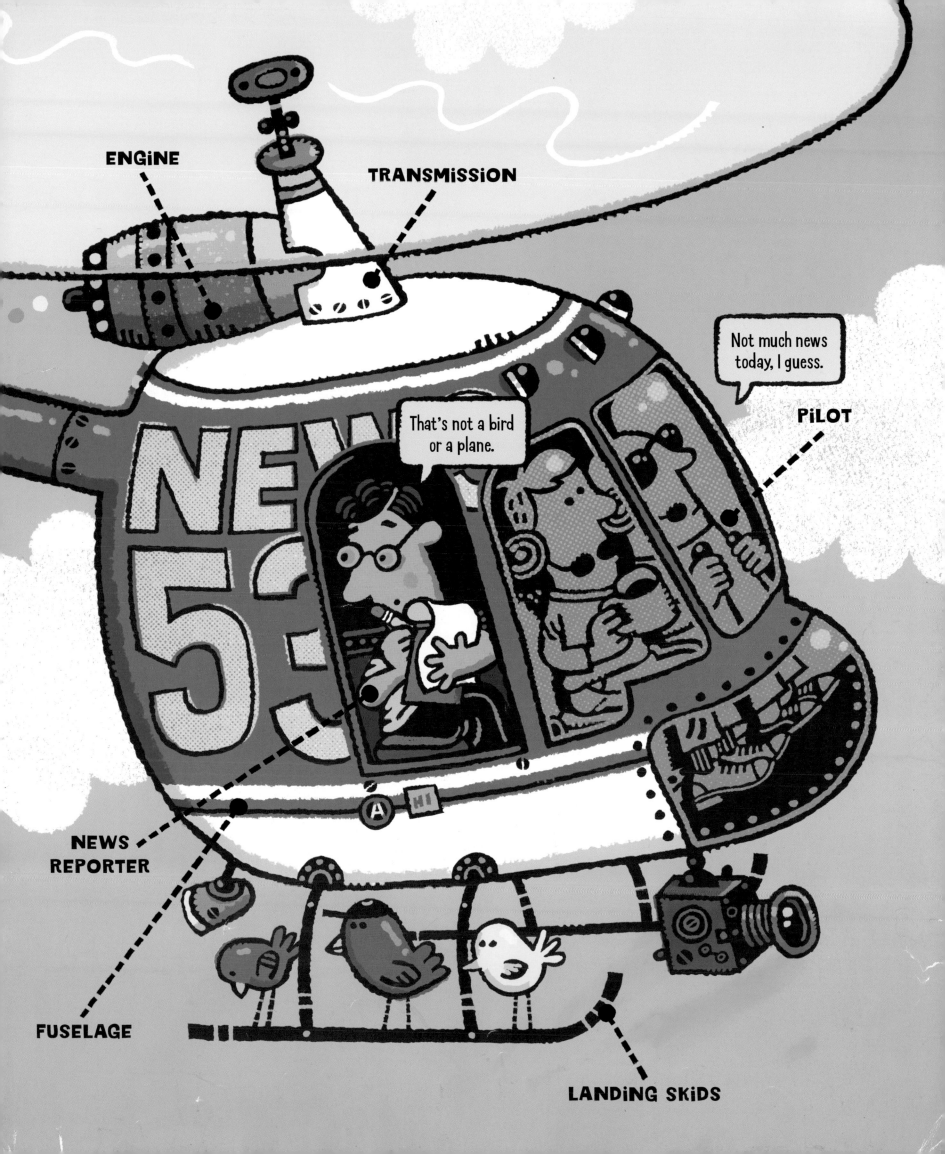

ENVELOPE

MOORING

ELEVATOR

YB65

YUM
ICE CREAM

RUDDER

ENGINE

Balloons use hot air to rise, and blimps use a gas called helium. Hot air and helium are both lighter than the regular air that we breathe, which allows blimps and balloons to float.

How do they land?

LANDING
GEAR

GONDOLA

He
HELIUM

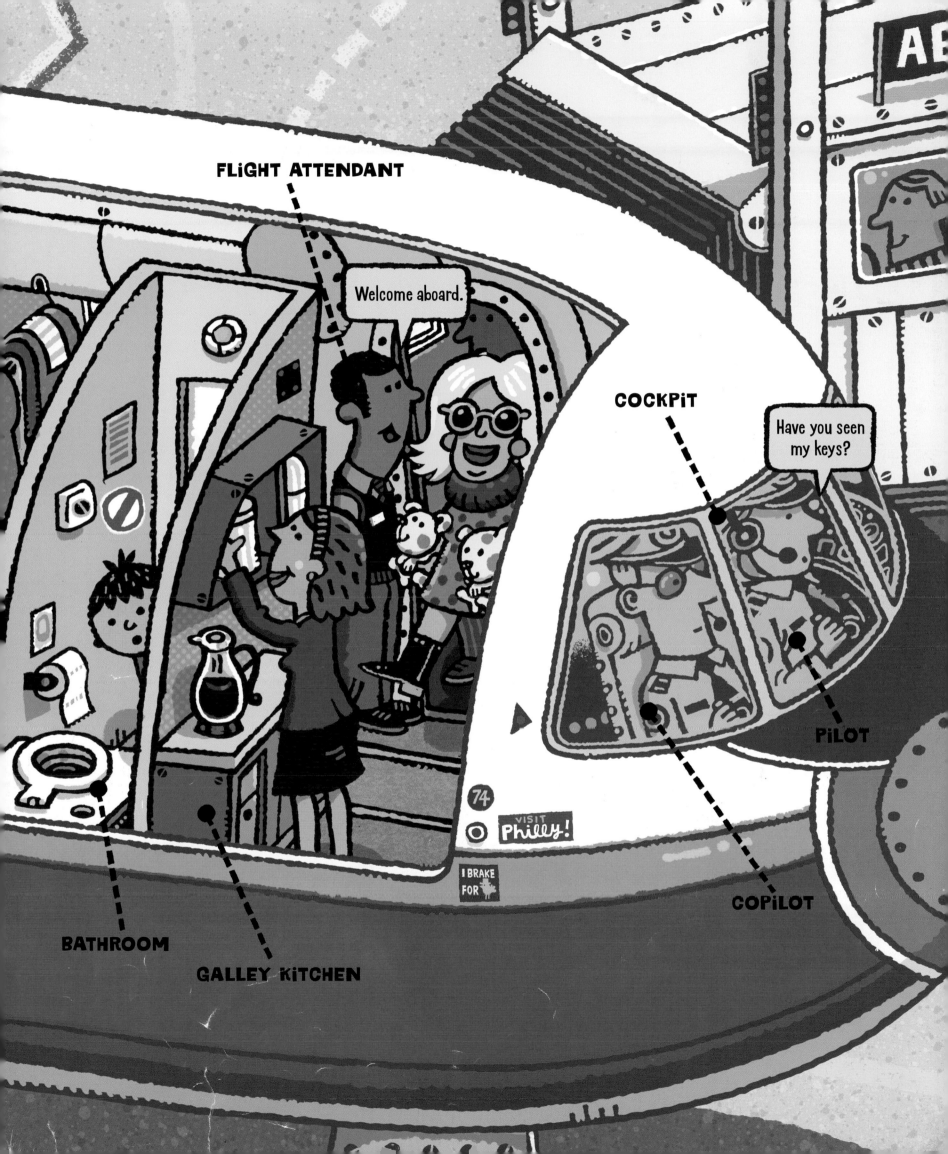

VARIOUS
INDICATORS
& GAUGES

THRUST
LEVER

PRIMARY FLIGHT
DISPLAY

YOKE

Some things about it are similar. Pilots have controls for steering the airplane and for speeding up and slowing down, and they have instruments that show the speed of the plane. But pilots also have to know how high they're flying, and whether they're going up or down, and they need radar to know if there are other planes in the area. . . .

It's much more complicated than driving a car.